Dedicated to my amazing wife Marilyn, my rock, my world, my everything.

AN UNEXPECTE D LOVE STORY

Contents

Chapter 1 A Heart in Turmoil

Tom Hawthorne stood in the kitchen, meticulously arranging a bouquet of roses inside a vase. The smile plastered on his face was one that could only come from a man head over heels in love. A gentle tune escaped his lips as he hummed with the rhythm of his heart.

"Serena is going to love these," he thought, reminiscing about their six-month anniversary dinner planned for later that evening. Tom's positive qualities shone through like the morning sun, lovingly baking a cake and making sure everything was perfect for their special night.

As kind and caring as Tom was, his appearance had seen better days. His short brown hair, once neatly groomed, now looked unkempt and disheveled. His expressive green eyes seemed to plead for attention, hidden beneath the weight he'd gained in recent months. Tom, once a carefree man in his early 30s, had neglected his appearance, letting himself go in the comfort of his relationship with Serena.

"Hey, Tom!" a voice called out, interrupting his thoughts. It was Serena, all dolled up and ready to go out with her friends instead of Tom, completely forgetting it was their 6 month anniversary. Surveying the kitchen, she couldn't help but look in discomfort at the sight of her slightly rotund boyfriend, covered in flour while trying to frost the cake.

"Wow, Tom, you really went all out," Serena said, without any affection in her voice. "You know, I never pegged you as the domestic type."

"Only for you, my love," Tom replied, grinning sheepishly. He wiped his hands on his flour-covered "Kiss the Cook" apron, leaving behind a trail of multicolored frosting. "Just wait till you taste this cake. It's my famous triple layer chocolate explosion. You'll think I'm secretly moonlighting as a pastry chef."

"Yeah, I can wait," Serena replied, rolling her eyes. She stepped closer to inspect the flowers, twirling a curl of her long, wavy brunette hair absentmindedly. "Roses? How original."

"Hey now, they're a classic for a reason!" Tom defended, a mock pout forming on his lips. He tried hard to hide how hurt he was that she had forgotten their date and was going out without him on their anniversary.

"Alright, alright," Serena relented, leaning in to give him a quick peck on the cheek, leaving a lipstick mark on his flour-dusted face. "Thanks for the effort."

"Anything for you," Tom said sincerely, his green eyes glistening with affection. As he stood in the kitchen, surrounded by the chaos of his baking endeavors, Tom couldn't help but feel that despite his current doughy appearance and the challenges life threw at him, he had found something special in Serena. Or was he just kidding himself that she felt the same?

"Anyway, I have to get going. Jake and the girls are waiting for me," Serena said, glancing at her watch. Her tone was indifferent, and it stung Tom more than he cared to admit. He knew that Serena had been growing increasingly distant over the past few weeks, but he had hoped their anniversary might rekindle some of the initial spark they once shared.

"Okay," Tom replied, trying to keep his disappointment in check. "Have fun with Jake and your friends." He emphasized the name Jake, wondering why she was going out with her handsome personal trainer instead of him.

"Thanks, babe," Serena said, grabbing her purse from the counter. She hesitated for a moment, looking as if she wanted to say something more, but then simply shook her head and walked toward the door.

"Wait, Serena!" Tom called out, unable to hold back any longer. "Before you go, can we talk about... us?"

Serena sighed, pausing in the doorway. "Tom, now's really not a good time."

"Then when?" Tom implored, desperation creeping into his voice. "You've been so distant lately, and I don't know what's going on. I'm trying my best here, but I feel like I'm losing you."

"Fine," Serena snapped, turning to face him. "You want to know what's going on? I'm leaving you, Tom. For Jake."

The words hit Tom like a wrecking ball, shattering his world in an instant. He stared at her, dumbfounded, feeling as though his heart had been ripped from his chest.

"Jake?" he stammered. "Your gym coach? The guy with biceps bigger than my head?"

"Yep. Remember how you told me you worked in the City? I thought you were some rich trader who would give me the lavish lifestyle I deserved," Serena said coldly, her hazel eyes devoid of any emotion. "But nope, you're just some IT guy who works literally in the city."

"Serena, please," Tom begged, tears welling up in his expressive green eyes. "I love you. I thought we had something special."

"Maybe we did, once," Serena replied, her voice flat and uncaring. "But that's over now. Goodbye, Tom."

As she walked out, Tom sank to his knees, his face buried in his hands, unable to comprehend the devastating reality of losing the one he thought he loved.

"Was it all a lie?" Tom choked out between sobs. "Did she ever really love me?"

He glanced around his apartment, the once happy memories now tainted by betrayal and heartbreak. The framed photo of them at the London Eye seemed to mock him, their joyous smiles in the picture a cruel reminder of what he'd lost.

"Am I not good enough?" Tom wondered aloud, his self-esteem shattered. His unkempt brown hair and the extra weight he'd put on over the past few months suddenly felt like glaring flaws that Serena must have despised.

As the tears continued to flow, Tom found himself spiraling into a pit of Rocky Road ice cream and despair. He questioned every aspect of his life, from his boring IT job to his doughy appearance, and couldn't help but feel like a failure. It was as if the light had gone out, leaving him alone and lost in the darkness.

As the days and nights passed, Tom tried to pull himself out of the depressive comfort eating state he was in.

"Pull yourself together, Tom," he whispered to himself, trying to muster up a shred of hope. "Maybe this is your chance to start over, to become the person you've always wanted to be."

But the pain of losing Serena still clung to him like melted chocolate chips to a spoon, tightening its grip around his heart like a vice. As much as he tried to focus on the potential for personal growth, Tom couldn't shake the feeling that he was a burnt biscuit beyond repair.

Just as Tom was about to sink further into a cookie dough abyss of despair, the front door swung open, revealing his loving parents, Caroline and Peter Hawthorne. They were an eccentric pair, two aged hippies who had always marched to the beat of their own bongo drum, filling Tom's life with laughter, love, and tofu meatloaf surprises.

"Tom, darling," Caroline said, her eyes brimming with concern as she took in her son's disheveled, frosting-covered appearance. "We heard what happened. Are you alright?"

Peter stepped forward, placing a reassuring hand on Tom's shoulder, accidentally getting it sticky. "We've never been fond of Serena, son. She was too shallow for someone like you, who has so much depth and kindness."

"Your father's right," Caroline chimed in, stroking Tom's unkempt hair affectionately. "You deserve someone who sees your true worth and loves you for who you are, not just what they think you can give them."

Their words of comfort and encouragement began to seep through the cracks in Tom's battered self-esteem, providing a glimmer of hope amid the darkness. "Maybe you're right," he admitted, wiping away his tears and leaving behind a smudged, chocolaty mess on his face. "Maybe I do deserve better."

"Of course you do!" Peter exclaimed, giving Tom a hearty pat on the back that left another sticky handprint. "And now is the perfect time for you to take control of your life and work on becoming the best version of yourself."

The seed of transformation had been planted, and as Tom contemplated his parents' advice, he couldn't help but feel a spark of determination flicker within him, as weak as a trick birthday candle but still aglow with hope.

The next day, still nursing his emotional rocky road ice cream wounds, Tom found himself sprawled across the couch, listlessly flipping through TV channels. As he landed on the lottery draw, he perked up slightly – it was a weekly ritual for Tom to check if his long-standing "lucky numbers" of 4-8-15-16-23-42 would finally bring him some fortune.

"Got it," Tom muttered as the first number was announced, barely registering the coincidence. The second and third numbers matched as well. "Got it! Got it!" he repeated, beginning to sit up as excitement grew.

With each subsequent number, Tom's excitement increased exponentially, his heart pounding in his chest. He could hardly believe it when the final number aligned with his ticket – he had just won the £6 million jackpot!

"Is this really happening?" Tom thought, clutching the winning ticket with trembling, sticky hands. In that moment, everything seemed possible, and he knew it was time to embark on the journey of self-improvement that his parents had encouraged.

Little did Tom know that this unexpected stroke of luck would be the catalyst for a life-changing adventure filled with laughter, self-discovery, quirky characters, maybe even romance, and plenty of surprises along the way.

With newfound determination and a stroke of incredible luck behind him, Tom decided to go all in on his journey of self-improvement. He resolved to travel incognito to California, where he would search for a fitness coach and life coach to help mold him into the confident and attractive man he knew he could become.

"Caroline, Peter," Tom announced, standing tall in front of his parents. "I've decided to take your advice to heart and invest in myself. I'm going to California to find a coach who can help me transform my life."

Caroline and Peter exchanged knowing glances before beaming at their son. "Tom, we're so proud of you!" Caroline gushed, her eyes welling up with happy tears. "You're taking control of your life, and we know you'll come out stronger on the other side."

"Thanks, Mum, Dad," Tom replied, grateful for their unwavering support. As he packed his bags, he couldn't help but feel a mixture of excitement and nervousness. This was it – he was leaving behind his old life and embarking on a fresh start.

The moment Tom boarded the plane to California, he could already feel the weight of his past lifting off his shoulders. He glanced out the window as the plane soared above the clouds, and his thoughts drifted to the days ahead. Would he find the perfect coach? Would his transformation lead to a new and fulfilling life?

"Focus, Tom," he whispered to himself. "You've got a long journey ahead, but it'll be worth it." With that thought firmly planted in his mind, Tom leaned back in his seat, brimming with hope and determination.

As the plane touched down in sunny California, Tom felt a surge of excitement wash over him. This was just the beginning of an unforgettable journey filled with laughter, self-discovery, and perhaps even love. And as he stepped off the plane and breathed in the fresh Californian air, Tom knew that his new life was waiting for him – all he had to do was embrace it and keep the truth about his good luck to himself.

Tom's first order of business was to test out potential life and fitness coaches, and he eagerly perused the profiles of various colorful candidates at gyms in the area.

"Just be cool, you've got this," Tom muttered to himself as he entered the first gym on his list, trying not to gawk at the ripped, glistening physiques around him. He hesitantly approached the front desk where a muscle-bound man sporting a buzzcut was typing away.

"Welcome to Muscle Mecca, what can I do for you?" the man grunted without looking up.

"Hi there, I'm Tom," he stammered, intimidated by the guy's massive biceps. "I'm looking for a personal trainer to help me get in shape?" He posed it as a question, suddenly feeling small and out of place.

The man finally glanced up, scanning Tom's soft physique with a critical eye. "Hmm, looks like you got some work to do," he remarked. "Go speak with Rico, he's got an opening. Good luck!"

Tom wandered into the weight room, scanning the area for this mysterious Rico. Suddenly a short but beastly muscular bald man appeared in front of him. "I'm Rico. You must be Tommy!" he shouted in an aggressive Italian accent.

"Oh, uh, hi Rico, I'm Tom-"

"No time for chit-chat! We must get to work!" Rico interrupted, blowing his whistle aggressively. "Now drop and give me one hundred push-ups!"

"Wait, what? I've never even done one-" Tom tried to protest but was cut off again.

"No excuses! Down! Now!" Rico commanded, forcing Tom to the ground.

As Tom struggled to squeak out even one shaky push-up, he thought in despair, maybe this Rico guy was a bit too intense for him...

The next day, Tom woke up sore in places he didn't know existed. The intense session with his drill sergeant trainer Rico had left him barely able to move.

"Today's the day," Tom groaned as he forced himself out of bed. "I'm going to find someone who can help me get fit without killing me."

After a soothing ice bath to reanimate his aching muscles, Tom found himself hesitantly approaching a gym called Mind and Body Fitness. Maybe this place would have someone a bit less aggressive than Rico, he hoped.

"Hello!" chirped the cheery receptionist. "Welcome to Mind and Body. Are you here for a session?"

Before Tom could answer, a lanky, bearded man in tight yoga pants and a man-bun emerged from the back room. "Namaste, friend. I'm Brock, your Mind and Body guide. Follow me."

As Brock led him to a small studio smelling of incense, Tom felt hopeful. This definitely wasn't another Rico situation.

"Now, we begin in mountain pose," Brock said in a soothing voice. They stood with arms raised as pan flute music played. Tom started to relax and follow Brock's graceful, fluid movements.

"Release the tension...feel your breath...empty your mind..." Brock guided them through gentle poses. Tom's muscles, still sore from Rico's relentless regimen, thanked him.

After an hour of tranquil stretching, Tom lay in final resting pose feeling more zen than ever. Maybe mind and body fitness was his thing after all.

Suddenly, Brock clapped loudly, jolting Tom from his relaxed state. "Alright, time to pump it up! Let's crush some cardio!" Brock yelled, abruptly turning on an EDM workout playlist.

Before Tom could react, Brock was doing high-knees and blasting the weights at record speed. "Feel the burn!" he shouted over thumping beats.

Tom stared in shock at the sudden change. "Wait, what's happening?" he exclaimed, but Brock couldn't hear him over the blaring music.

As Brock leapt about rapidly, loose weights flying, Tom ducked for cover. "Downward dog to leg lifts...now jumping burpees!" Brock hollered.

Tom scrambled out of the gym, collapsing onto the smoothie bar. Maybe mind and body fitness wasn't so balanced after all...

Tom stumbled out of Mind and Body Fitness feeling defeated. He had struck out again in his attempt to find a trainer who could help mold him into the man he wanted to become.

Another day down but with renewed determination, Tom set off on the next step of his quirky coaching journey, ready for whatever offbeat mentor might come his way next. Hey, he'd already won the lottery - finding the right coach couldn't be that hard, could it?

Tom checked his list and saw his next interview was with Samantha Greene. Approaching her office, he noticed a poster on the door showing raw vegetables and the slogan "Raw is Life."

"Here goes nothing," Tom muttered, knocking.

"Come in!" came a stern voice.

Tom entered and was met by a tall, slender woman with piercing eyes that scrutinized him.

"I'm Samantha Greene," she said tightly. "Have a seat."

"Thanks," Tom replied, sitting nervously.

"Let's get right to it," Samantha began briskly. "I advocate a strict raw food diet - no processed or cooked foods, no animal products. Are you willing to fully commit?"

Tom swallowed. He'd never been a health nut but was open to trying new things. "Well, I'm willing to give it a go," he said hesitantly.

Samantha raised an eyebrow. "You think you can handle it? I've seen many crumble under the demands of true health."

"I just need guidance and support to improve myself," Tom explained.

Samantha considered him critically before agreeing, "Fine, but be warned - the path to health requires discipline and determination. Are you prepared?"

"I am," Tom nodded, trying to seem confident.

"Good. Let's begin," Samantha said coolly.

As they continued, Tom felt discouraged by her strict requirements. But he was determined to see this through , how hard could some kale smoothies be?

Suddenly, they were interrupted by a loud commotion outside. Tom opened the door to find an angry mob waving signs saying "We Want Real Food!" A smiling man walked up to Tom and introduced himself as the leader of the Processed Food Lovers Union there to protest Samantha's raw-only approach. Tom looked back uncertainly at Samantha's shocked face. Well, he thought, looks like finding the right coach just got a whole lot more complicated!

"Get out of here, you junk food fanatics!" Samantha yelled at the protesters, her face red with anger. "You're just jealous because you lack the self-control to lead a healthy lifestyle!"

"Healthy? More like tasteless and boring!" retorted the leader of the Processed Food Lovers Union. The crowd behind him cheered, waving their signs with enthusiasm.

Tom stood in the middle of the chaos, feeling utterly overwhelmed. As much as he wanted to find a coach who could help him change his life, he didn't want to get caught in the crossfire of dietary warfare. He glanced at Samantha, whose eyes were ablaze with fury, and realized that maybe her raw food regimen wasn't quite for him either. After all, he loved the occasional burger and chips as much as the next person.

"Uh, Samantha," Tom said hesitantly, trying to be heard over the commotion. "I appreciate your willingness to help me, but I think I need to keep looking for someone who's more... well, balanced."

"Balanced?" Samantha scoffed. "Fine, go back to your unhealthy ways. But don't come crying to me when you realize you've made a terrible mistake!"

"Thank you for your time," Tom replied, backing away slowly before turning on his heel and retreating from the scene.

As he walked away from Samantha's house and the ongoing protest, Tom couldn't shake the feeling of disappointment that weighed him down. Maybe finding the perfect coach was an impossible task. He began to doubt if he would ever find someone who truly understood his needs and could guide him on this journey of self-improvement.

"Chin up, Tom," he reminded himself, taking a deep breath. "There have to be other coaches out there. You just need to keep looking."

With renewed determination, Tom decided to continue his search, hoping against hope that the right person was just around the corner. All he needed was a bit of luck and maybe, just maybe, he would find the coach who could help him transform his life for good.

A name caught his eye: Jordan Taylor, a life and fitness coach who specialized in helping people overcome personal obstacles and reach their full potential. The description sounded promising, and after reading through a few glowing testimonials, Tom felt a flicker of hope.

"Alright, Jordan Taylor, here goes nothing," he muttered, dialing the number listed on the website. The call went to voicemail, and Tom left a message explaining his situation and requesting a callback.

As the days passed with no reply from Jordan, Tom's optimism began to wane. He tried reaching out to other coaches, but each one seemed to be either too busy or not quite the right fit for his needs. His discouragement grew, and he wondered if maybe he was simply meant to remain stuck in his current state, unable to break free from the chains of self-doubt and insecurity.

"Maybe this whole journey was a mistake," Tom thought dejectedly as he sat on his couch, going over his ever-shrinking list of potential coaches. He could feel the weight of loneliness settling over him like a heavy blanket, and he longed for the warmth and support of his parents, Caroline and Peter.

"Tom, lad," his father's voice echoed in his memory, "you've got to keep believing in yourself, even when it feels like the world is against you."

"Your father's right, dear," his mother chimed in. "You have to take control of your life and work on your self-improvement. Believe me, it's worth it."

Tom closed his eyes, drawing strength from the memories of his parents' unwavering support. He knew they were right; he couldn't give up on himself so easily.

Chapter 2 the Journey Begins

Tom stood in the entrance of yet another gym, his heart sinking as he looked around at the array of equipment and spandex-clad fitness enthusiasts. He knew he had to do something about his expanding waistline, but so far, his search for a personal trainer had been an exercise in futility. He was about to give up when the gym manager walked over with a young woman in tow.

"Tom, I'd like you to meet Emma Sullivan," the manager said, gesturing to the woman beside him. "She's one of our best trainers."

Emma extended her hand confidently, her firm grip surprising Tom. Her striking brown eyes held his gaze, leaving no room for doubt that she meant business. Her athletic build and shoulder-length black hair gave her a strong, powerful aura that demanded respect as most Latino women did that Tom had met since arriving in California.

"Nice to meet you, Tom." Emma's voice was warm yet resolute. "I've heard you're looking to make some serious changes to your life. Let me assure you, I'm the one who can help you achieve those goals."

Tom hesitated, eyeing the kettlebells and battle ropes warily. "Well, I don't know if I'd say 'serious' changes… maybe just a little, uh, fine-tuning?" He chuckled nervously, trying to downplay his current state of unfitness.

"Fine-tuning?" Emma raised an eyebrow, clearly not amused by Tom's attempt at humor. "Tom, you came here because you want to change. And I'll be honest – it's going to take more than just a few tweaks here and there. My methods are tough, but they work. Are you ready for that?"

Tom's shoulders slumped, and he avoided her piercing gaze. He wasn't used to such directness, and part of him wanted to run for the hills. But there was something about Emma's unwavering confidence that intrigued him, her tough-love approach a challenge he hadn't expected.

"Look, I'm not going to sugarcoat it," Emma continued, crossing her arms. "You're going to work hard, and there will be moments when you'll want to quit. But I promise you, if you stick with me and trust the process, you'll see results."

Tom glanced around the gym once more, taking in the determined faces of the people working out. Could he really do this? Could he become one of them? He thought about his parents, Caroline and Peter, always supportive but undoubtedly worried about his recent weight gain and lack of self-care.

"Alright," Tom finally said, meeting Emma's eyes. "I don't know what it is about you, but... I'll give it a shot. Let's do this."

"Great!" Emma clapped her hands together, her face breaking into a smile that softened her previously stern expression. "I won't let you down, Tom. And I know you won't let yourself down, either."

As Tom followed her towards the weights section, he couldn't help but feel a spark of hope ignite within him. Maybe, just maybe, Emma was the key to unlocking the change he so desperately sought.

"Let's start with basics to assess your fitness," Emma said, clipboard ready. "Give me push-ups till failure."

Tom scanned for an escape. "You know, I've heard push-ups can cause premature wrinkling," he joked desperately. "Wouldn't want that!"

Emma's eyebrow shot up. "Nice try. No more stalling, drop and give me twenty...or however many you can manage."

Sighing heavily, Tom shakily lowered himself. As he struggled through each rep, sweat poured down his forehead. At rep three, his noodle arms started trembling dangerously. Emily watched, unimpressed.

At rep five, he let out an exaggerated groan worthy of an Olympic weightlifter. At rep seven, his face went redder than a tomato. Finally, he collapsed at rep nine, gasping for air.

"Let's be generous and call that ten," Emma said, scribbling on her clipboard.

"Phew...you don't start...easy," Tom panted.

"If it was easy, you wouldn't need me. Now on your feet for lunges!"

Emma demonstrated perfect form. Tom tried copying her, wobbling like a newborn deer.

"Really feel the burn!" Emma enthused.

"Oh, I'm feeling it alright," Tom grimaced, hobbling pitifully.

Just then, "Eye of the Tiger" blared on the stereo.

"Yeah! Let's lunge to this!" Emma shouted, aggressively pumping her fists. Tom stared bewildered as she sang along, kicking and lunging wildly.

Gym members stopped and stared. Tom face-palmed, shrinking away in embarrassment.

"Come on, Tom, feel the beat!" Emma yelled.

"On second thought, I just remembered an important doctor's appointment!" Tom yelped, hightailing it for the exit.

Emma blinked in surprise as Tom barreled out the door. Well, she thought, looks like I might need to dial it down a notch with this one!

"Hey, Tom! Wait up!" Emma called out as she raced after him in the parking lot.

Tom slowed down, panting heavily. "You know, I think I liked you better when you were just singing and dancing," he wheezed.

"Sorry about that. I got a bit carried away. Let's have a chat instead, alright?" Emma suggested, guiding Tom to a nearby bench where they both sat down.

"Alright, I'm game. But if you break into song again, I'm out of here," Tom said with a weak attempt at humor.

"Deal." Emma smiled. "Here's the thing, Tom. My coaching philosophy is simple: I push you hard because I believe in you. I know it's tough, but I've seen people like you make incredible transformations."

"Really? You think I can turn into one of those guys with abs you could grate cheese on?" Tom asked skeptically, rubbing his belly.

"Maybe not overnight, but with hard work and dedication, yes. It's not just about physical appearance; it's about improving your self-confidence and overall well-being. We'll focus on fitness routines, diet, and mindset shifts."

"Mindset shifts? You mean like Jedi mind tricks?" Tom joked, waving his hand in front of her face.

"More like learning to embrace challenges and replace negative thoughts with positive ones," Emma clarified, rolling her eyes playfully. "But if you want to pretend you're a Jedi while you're at it, be my guest."

"Right, well, if I'm going to be a Jedi, I need a teacher who's tough enough to whip me into shape. Someone who won't let me quit even when I feel like giving up. Someone like you, maybe?" Tom said hesitantly, his voice wavering slightly as he revealed a flicker of vulnerability.

Emma looked into Tom's expressive green eyes and saw the determination hidden beneath the humor. It was in that moment that she knew she could help him.

"Tom, if you're willing to trust me and commit to this journey, I promise I'll be with you every step of the way. And who knows? We might even have a laugh or two along the way," Emma said, offering her hand.

"Alright, Coach Emma, you've got yourself a deal. Let's do this!" Tom declared, shaking her hand firmly.

As they walked back inside the gym, Tom couldn't help but feel a sense of hope bubbling within him. Maybe, just maybe, Emma's tough-love approach was exactly what he needed to make a positive change in his life.

"Alright, Tom. We start tomorrow," Emma said decisively, already making mental notes of what their first session would be like. "And remember, this is a journey – not just about losing weight, but also about rediscovering who you are and what you're capable of."

"Got it, Coach," Tom replied with a nod, feeling both nervous and excited at the prospect of embarking on this transformative journey.

"Good. Now, before we begin, I want you to set some goals for yourself," Emma instructed. "Think about what you want to achieve, not just physically but mentally as well."

"Right, so, lose weight, gain confidence, and maybe even learn how to do a handstand?" Tom suggested, half-jokingly.

Emma chuckled. "That's a good start, but let's dig deeper. Why do you want to lose weight? What will that enable you to do?"

Tom paused to consider her question. "I guess... I want to feel better about myself. To be able to look in the mirror and be proud of the person I see. And maybe be the person my ex would want to get back with.

"Sounds like solid goals to me," Emma nodded, impressed by his honesty. "Now, are you willing to put in the work to achieve them?"

"Absolutely," Tom replied, his eagerness evident in his voice. "I'm ready to give it everything I've got."

"Great! Then let's get started tomorrow, 6.00am!" Emma exclaimed, clapping her hands together.

"Six in the morning?" Tom groaned, his enthusiasm waning for a moment. "You're not kidding about the no-nonsense thing, are you?"

"Tom, success doesn't wait for anyone, especially when it comes to transforming your life," Emma replied firmly. "Now, let's talk about our plan. We'll begin with a mix of cardio and strength training sessions. I want you to build endurance and muscle tone."

"Cardio and strength? Sounds like a party," Tom said sarcastically, masking his anxiety with humor.

"Trust me, it'll be worth it," Emma assured him. "We'll also work on dietary changes. Clean eating, portion control, and meal planning will be essential to fuel your body properly for our workouts."

"Goodbye, late-night kebabs," Tom sighed, but there was determination in his eyes.

"Exactly," Emma nodded, pleased with his resolve. "Lastly, we'll focus on mindset shifts. You need to believe in yourself and develop a positive attitude towards this journey. No more self-deprecating jokes, okay?"

"Okay, I'll try," Tom agreed, knowing his penchant for using humor as a defense mechanism would be a tough habit to break.

The next day, at 6:00 am sharp, Tom met Emma at the gym, bleary-eyed but determined. As they began their first workout together, Tom quickly realized just how challenging this transformation would be. He struggled through the cardio exercises, gasping for breath and drenched in sweat. The strength training proved equally difficult, with his muscles trembling under the strain of weights he'd never attempted before.

"Come on, Tom! You can do this!" Emma encouraged him, her voice both stern and supportive.

"Easy for you to say," Tom grunted between labored breaths, trying to keep up with her relentless pace.

"Remember what we talked about, Tom. Positive mindset," she reminded him.

"Right, positive thoughts," he panted, forcing a smile. "I love the burn. I love the sweat. And I especially love the feeling of my soul leaving my body."

"Progress," Emma grinned, knowing that humor would always be a part of Tom's charm. But beneath his jokes, she could see the determination in his eyes, and she knew he was ready to face the challenges ahead. Together, they would embark on this transformative journey, one step at a time.

Over the next few weeks, Tom and Emma continued their intense workout sessions, each day pushing Tom to his limits. But with every passing day, he noticed small improvements – a little more stamina, a bit more strength, and gradually, the numbers on the scale started to decrease as well.

"Keep going, Tom! You're doing great!" Emma shouted over the pounding of their feet on the treadmills.

"Thanks," Tom replied, his chest heaving as he tried to maintain his pace. "I couldn't have done it without you."

Emma smiled in response, her eyes filled with pride. She knew that Tom had what it took to succeed, but seeing him put in the effort and start to believe in himself was incredibly rewarding.

As they worked together, Tom began to trust Emma's guidance more and more. Her no-nonsense approach, which had initially been intimidating, now seemed exactly what he needed to keep him focused and motivated. And as his body transformed, so too did his mindset. He began to embrace the challenges rather than shy away from them, recognizing that growth happened outside of his comfort zone.

"Alright, Tom, last set of squats. You've got this!" Emma encouraged him, her voice firm yet supportive.

"Here goes nothing," he muttered, bending his knees and lowering himself down. As he pushed back up, sweat dripping from his brow, he felt a sense of accomplishment wash over him. His legs were stronger, his form was better, and the exercise that had once left him gasping for breath now felt almost manageable.

"Great job today, Tom," Emma said as they finally wrapped up their session. "You've really come a long way."

"Thanks, Emma," Tom replied, wiping his face with a towel. "I couldn't have done it without you. You believed in me when I didn't even believe in myself."

"Of course," she replied, her eyes shining with sincerity. "I knew you had it in you all along."

As Tom took a moment to reflect on his progress, he couldn't help but feel grateful for Emma's unwavering support. She had been there for him every step of the way, pushing him to be better, and helping him discover a strength he never knew he had. For the first time in a long time, Tom felt truly optimistic about the future – and excited to see what more they could accomplish together.

One evening after an intense workout session, Tom and Emma decided to take a break and go for a walk around the park. The sun was setting, casting a warm glow over their faces as they strolled side by side. Laughter came easily between them, as they shared stories of their lives outside the gym.

"Did I ever tell you about the time I accidentally set my kitchen on fire trying to make toast?" Tom asked, grinning sheepishly.

"Toast? How did you manage that?" Emma laughed, intrigued.

"Let's just say I got distracted and forgot about it," Tom admitted, chuckling at the memory. "My parents still won't let me live it down."

"Sounds like something I would do," Emma confessed, her eyes dancing with amusement. "We can be disaster chefs together."

As they continued swapping stories, Tom couldn't help but notice how much more comfortable and open he felt in Emma's presence. She wasn't just his coach – she had become a true friend, someone he could trust and rely on.

"Emma, I just wanted to say thank you," Tom said earnestly, looking into her striking brown eyes. "Not just for helping me get healthier, but for being there for me emotionally too. You've been such an amazing friend, and I'm so grateful to have you in my life."

"Tom, I'm grateful for you too," Emma replied, touched by his words. "You've shown me that it's okay to let my guard down and be vulnerable with someone. And I'm proud of the progress we've made together."

As they stood there, bathed in the golden light of the setting sun, Tom knew that he was not only transforming physically but mentally as well. With Emma by his side, he felt like he could conquer any challenge that came his way. Their deepening bond fueled his determination, and he eagerly looked forward to the next stage of their journey together.

"Alright, enough with the mushy stuff," Emma teased, playfully poking Tom in his now-toned stomach. "We've still got work to do."

"Of course, Coach Sullivan," Tom replied with a smirk, knowing full well that she was trying to keep things lighthearted even though she too appreciated their bond. "What's next on our transformative agenda?"

"Actually, I've been thinking about incorporating some new activities into our routine," Emma said, her eyes twinkling with excitement. "I want to challenge you even more and help you uncover new strengths."

"Sounds intriguing," Tom said, curiosity piqued. "What kind of activities?"

"First, we're going to give rock climbing a try," Emma announced, grinning at Tom's wide-eyed reaction. "It'll test your physical strength and mental fortitude. Plus, it's an incredible workout."

"Rock climbing?!" Tom exclaimed, his heart racing at the thought of scaling a wall. He had never considered attempting such a feat before, but this newfound confidence in himself made him eager to give it a shot.

"Absolutely! And then we'll explore other fun activities like dance classes, yoga, and maybe even join a local sports league," Emma added, her enthusiasm infectious. "We're not just focused on the gym – we're creating a well-rounded, active lifestyle for you."

"Wow, those all sound fantastic," Tom admitted, his initial hesitation fading as he embraced the idea of expanding his horizons. "You know what? Let's do it! Sign me up for everything!"

"Really?" Emma asked, pleasantly surprised by Tom's eagerness.

"Really," Tom confirmed, his voice filled with conviction. "I'm all in, Emma. I trust you, and I believe in the path we're taking. So, let's make some positive changes and enjoy every step of the way."

"Then let's get started!" Emma said, her warm smile signaling her pride in Tom's commitment. As they walked away from the park hand in hand, Tom couldn't help but feel a surge of excitement for all the possibilities that lay ahead.

Together, they were an unstoppable team, and Tom knew that with Emma's guidance and their shared determination, there was no limit to the positive changes he could make in his life.

The next morning, Tom met Emma at the rock climbing gym, trying his best to mask his nerves with humor.

"Well, I wore my extra grippy socks today, so this wall doesn't stand a chance," he joked, staring up at the imposing 50-foot wall dotted with multi-colored holds.

Emma laughed, giving him an encouraging pat on the back. "Don't worry, we'll start on the beginner walls first. I'll be belaying and spotting you the whole time."

She helped Tom into the harness and expertly tied the ropes. As Tom gingerly approached the wall, Emma gave him a detailed tutorial on footwork, hand placement, and body positioning.

Tom tentatively reached for the first vibrant blue hold, his foot slipping on the textured wall. He dangled awkwardly until Emma stabilized him.

"Keep your weight centered! You got this!" she called out. Tom gritted his teeth and tried again, managing a few wobbly moves upwards.

"I feel like one of those sticky-handed toys kids throw at walls, except a lot less sticky," Tom quipped through labored breaths.

After an exhausting first attempt, Tom sat down, massaging his forearms. "Wow, I had no idea climbing used so many different muscles. My arms are jelly!"

"It's a full body workout for sure," Emma agreed. "But it also builds mental strength and courage. Pushing your limits, trusting yourself and your partner - it's incredibly empowering."

Tom nodded, contemplating her words. She was right - although physically demanding, the mental aspect intrigued him.

"Alright, I'm ready to try again," he declared, re-chalking his hands.

Over the next hour, Tom slowly gained confidence, relying on Emma's guidance to improve his technique. By the end, he had scaled halfway up the wall, beaming with pride.

"Great job! I knew you had it in you," Emma said.

"I couldn't have done it without my trusty belayer," Tom replied gratefully.

As they continued attending rock climbing sessions, Tom noticed the activity becoming easier, almost meditative. The laser focus required helped quiet his usual self-doubt, leaving only clarity of purpose.

Soon after, Emma and Tom ventured into a dance studio, the mirrored walls and barres contrasting the rugged cliffs.

As the instructor demonstrated complex Latin dance steps, Tom stared, dumbfounded. "Um, I should warn you that I have two left feet. And ankles. And knees," he stage-whispered to Emma.

She simply laughed, gracefully pulling him to his feet. "Just follow my lead!"

Tom stumbled through the cha-cha, desperately glancing at the instructor's feet to mimic the steps. Emma maintained steady eye contact, guiding him patiently across the studio, her body swaying in time to the upbeat music.

"Ow!" Tom yelped as Emma's heel collided with his toes.

"Whoops, sorry!" Emma said. "You okay?"

"Yep, all good!" Tom said through gritted teeth. After a quick breather, he rejoined Emma with renewed concentration.

By the end of the class, Tom managed to string together a few semi-graceful sequences. His technique needed work, but he had successfully tried something entirely new and challenging.

Over the next few weeks, Emma continued surprising Tom with exciting new activities - paddleboarding, salsa dancing, acro-yoga. Each one pushed him in different ways, building physical strength, flexibility, balance, and courage.

Of course, hilarious mishaps occurred frequently. Attempting acro-yoga, Tom toppled over, squashing Emma in an undignified tangle of limbs. During salsa class, he accidentally whipped Emma with a flamboyant arm move, almost knocking her off her feet. And paddleboarding left them both drenched after capsizing into the lake multiple times.

But the laughter and camaraderie strengthened their bond. Each activity became an opportunity for growth and playfulness. And Tom noticed a growing self-assurance replacing his previous uncertainty.

One day, as they shared a post-workout smoothie, Tom turned to Emma. "You know, when we started this whole thing, I was terrified. I thought I'd fail miserably at any physical activity. But you've pushed me to try things I never imagined possible, and somehow it's worked! I can't believe the progress I've made, thanks to you."

Emma smiled warmly. "You're giving me too much credit. Ultimately, you decided to commit to this journey and put in the hard work. I just gave you a friendly nudge now and then."

"A nudge? More like a full-on shove out of my comfort zone," Tom chuckled. "But really, I needed that. You've helped me discover strength and courage I didn't know I had in me."

Tom raised his smoothie glass. "Here's to an amazing coach, mentor, and friend. You've changed my life, Emma."

"Cheers!" Emma replied, clinking her glass with Tom's. "Now, ready for sand volleyball next week?"

Tom grinned excitedly. With Emma by his side, he was ready for whatever thrilling adventure awaited.

Chapter 3 Building The Body

Tom, beads of sweat dripping down his flushed face, grunted as he completed yet another repetition with the barbell. His green eyes were laser-focused on the gym mirror in front of him, watching himself push through the pain and strain of each lift. The once carefree man had found a new sense of purpose in his early 30s – a determination to transform himself mentally and physically.

"Come on, Tom! You can do it!" He whispered encouragingly to himself, his unkempt brown hair sticking to his forehead. With every muscle in his body trembling, Tom managed to complete one final rep before gently placing the barbell back onto the rack. He let out a deep sigh of relief, feeling the burn from head to toe.

As he wiped away the perspiration with a towel, Tom couldn't help but feel a sense of pride swelling within him. He knew he had come a long way since first stepping foot into this gym, and the changes in his appearance were becoming increasingly noticeable.

At the other end of the gym, Emma Sullivan leaned against a treadmill, her striking brown eyes observing Tom's progress discreetly from a distance. Her shoulder-length black hair was pulled back into a tight ponytail, revealing the subtle curve of her strong jawline. As a life coach and personal trainer, Emma had seen many clients give up and crumble under the pressure of their goals. But not Tom. She admired his unwavering dedication and how he pushed himself to his limits with every workout.

Emma crossed her arms over her lean, athletic figure and smiled softly to herself. She couldn't deny that her feelings for Tom were growing stronger by the day. There was something about his genuine nature and newfound determination that tugged at her heartstrings. Even though they had grown close during their training sessions, she knew there was still an emotional barrier between them – one that she couldn't quite break through just yet.

"Keep up the good work, Tom!" Emma called out from across the gym, trying to keep her tone casual and friendly. She knew that she couldn't let him see the depth of her feelings, not when he was still so focused on his journey of self-improvement.

"Thanks, Emma!" Tom replied with a smile, his green eyes lighting up at her praise. Little did he know that her admiration for him went beyond his physical transformation – it was his heart, his spirit, and his indomitable will that truly captivated her.

Emma decided it was time to approach Tom and offer him some words of encouragement. She walked over to where he was working out, her heart racing with every step.

"Tom, I just wanted to say that your progress is really impressive," she said as she stood beside him, subtly hinting at her feelings for him. "I've seen a lot of people struggle with their goals, but you're truly an inspiration."

"Thank you, Emma," Tom responded, genuinely grateful for her support. "I couldn't have done it without you. You've been such a great coach and friend throughout this whole process." He paused for a moment, his gaze lingering on Emma's striking brown eyes before continuing. "But you know what my real motivation is – winning Serena back."

Emma's heart sank at the mention of Serena, but she maintained her composure. "I know how important she is to you, Tom," she said, trying not to let her disappointment show. "And I'm sure she'll be blown away by your transformation when she sees you."

"Hopefully," Tom said, his voice filled with determination. "I have big plans to surprise her with the new me. I want to show her that I've changed, not just physically, but mentally too."

"Tom, just remember that you're doing this for yourself first and foremost," Emma advised, her voice soft and sincere. "It's wonderful that you want to win Serena back, but make sure you're proud of who you are, regardless of whether or not she appreciates it."

"Of course, Emma," Tom agreed, nodding his head. "Thanks again for all your help. I don't know what I'd do without you."

"Anytime, Tom," Emma replied, forcing a smile. As they exchanged glances, she wished more than ever that he could see what was right in front of him, but she knew that for now, her feelings would have to remain unspoken.

Their eyes met, and for a brief moment, time seemed to slow down. The unspoken connection between them hung heavy in the air, creating an almost palpable tension. It was as if their innermost thoughts and desires were on the verge of being revealed, but neither one dared to take that leap.

"Anyway," Tom said, breaking the lingering gaze. "I should get back to research. I want to plan something really special for Serena."

"Of course," Emma replied, her heart sinking once more. "Let me know if you need any help."

"Thanks, Emma," Tom said gratefully, and with that, he turned his attention back to his laptop.

As Tom went about his search for romantic gestures, Emma couldn't help but feel a twinge of envy for the woman who held Tom's affection so completely. He was pouring all his energy into winning Serena back, unaware of the feelings growing stronger within his closest confidant.

"Emma," Tom suddenly called out, looking up from his computer screen. "Can I tell you something? Something I haven't told anyone else?"

"Of course, Tom," Emma assured him, her curiosity piqued. "You can trust me."

He hesitated for a moment before taking a deep breath and saying, "I won the lottery just before I decided to come here and reinvent myself, a whopping £6,000,000." Tom paused, observing Emma's reaction. "I've kept it a secret, but I'm sure that with my new body and healthy bank account, Serena would want me back."

Emma's eyes widened in surprise, but she quickly masked her shock with a supportive smile. "Wow, Tom, that's amazing news!

Congratulations!" She hesitated, then added softly, "But don't forget that you deserve someone who loves you for who you are, not just for your outward appearance or wealth."

"Thanks, Emma," Tom said, his voice filled with gratitude. "I'll keep that in mind."

As Tom continued researching ideas for winning Serena back, Emma couldn't help but feel a growing frustration and sadness at being pushed aside. She knew she had to respect Tom's wishes, even if it meant watching him chase after someone who might never truly appreciate the incredible man he was, even before changing his physical appearance and becoming a millionaire.

"Emma," Tom suddenly said, breaking her out of her thoughts. "I have one final request before I head back to London. Would you help me with the last part of my transformation? You know, take me clothes shopping and get a new haircut? I want to make sure I'm looking my best for when I see Serena."

"Sure, Tom," Emma agreed, swallowing the knot in her throat. "I'd be happy to help." As they walked through the mall together, Emma couldn't help but feel torn between her own feelings for Tom and her respect for his wishes. She knew that Serena would likely come back to him, but not to the real Tom and not for the right reasons.

Emma and Tom strolled through the bustling mall together, chatting and laughing as they went from store to store. Tom emerged from each fitting room modeling various flashy outfits, eliciting giggles from Emma as she gave her honest opinions on each one. She was amazed by his willingness to try on anything she suggested, even if it was far outside his typical polished, buttoned-up style.

Though Emma tried to focus on their fun excursion, she couldn't ignore the bittersweet ache in her heart. With each adoring glance from Tom that made her blush, she was reminded that his affections were aimed at someone else. Still, she treasured their ability to talk for hours about everything under the sun. Tom's quirky jokes and unbridled enthusiasm never failed to lift her spirits.

At the salon, Emma watched as the stylist carefully trimmed Tom's shaggy locks and sharpened his look. She realized with awe that she was seeing glimpses of the man Tom was becoming - more vibrant, more carefree, more himself. When he turned to her with an uncertain expression, seeking her approval, she reassured him with a warm smile and a thumbs up.

By the time they left the mall, Tom walked taller, his eyes glinting with refreshed confidence. Emma's heart swelled with pride and admiration. Yet when he spoke of his grand plans to win back Serena, the ache returned. She now understood that her role was to guide him on this journey of growth and self-discovery. Even if it meant watching him give his heart to someone else, Emma resolved to savor their special bond while she still could.

"Alright," Tom announced, "time to plan the grand gesture to win Serena back. I think I'll need some help from my parents on this one."

When Tom video-called his parents Caroline and Peter, they were eager to learn more about the woman their son had been raving about in all his messages - Emma. As soon as she came into view on the screen, they understood his admiration. Her kind eyes and warm smile made it clear she cared deeply for their son.

"So this is the famous Emma we've heard so much about!" Caroline exclaimed. "It's lovely to finally meet you, dear."

Emma blushed. "The pleasure is mine, Mr. and Mrs. Hawthorne. Tom speaks very highly of you both."

As Tom excitedly shared his plans to win back Serena, his parents exchanged worried glances. They gently tried to steer the conversation towards learning more about his and Emma's adventures together. But Tom was too enthralled in his own grand ideas to notice their subtle hints.

"Well," Peter sighed, "if this is what will make you happy, son, your mother and I will support you however we can."

When the call ended, Caroline shook her head sadly. "Oh, I wish he could see what's right in front of him. That Emma is a gem."

Peter put his arm around his wife. "Unfortunately, this is a lesson our boy needs to learn for himself. We just have to trust that one day his eyes will open."

Emma hid her disappointment, knowing she had to keep supporting Tom on his journey, even if it meant silently yearning for his heart.

Over the next few days, Emma found herself growing increasingly frustrated and sad as she witnessed Tom's unwavering focus on Serena. She felt as though she was being pushed aside, all their time together seemingly forgotten in his quest to win back his ex-girlfriend. In spite of her feelings, Emma maintained a brave face and continued to help Tom with his plans.

One afternoon, they were sitting in a cafe discussing more romantic gestures for Serena when Emma could no longer contain her emotions. "Tom, can I ask you something?" she began hesitantly.

"Of course, Emma," he replied, putting down his notebook. "What's up?"

"Is this girl really worth all this effort after the way she hurt you?" Emma blurted out, her voice wavering slightly. "I mean, you've grown so much and become such an incredible person during our time together. Are you sure you want to go back to someone who couldn't appreciate you for who you were?"

Tom stared at her, taken aback by her sudden outburst. He had never considered that perhaps Serena wasn't the one he should be chasing after, especially not now that he had met someone like Emma.

"Emma, I..." he started, but was interrupted by her voice, trembling with emotion.

"Tom, I just... I care about you so much, and it breaks my heart to see you pouring your energy into someone who might not even deserve it." Her eyes filled with tears as she looked away, realizing she had come dangerously close to confessing her true feelings for him.

"Emma, I had no idea you felt this way," Tom stammered, equally confused and surprised by her words. A flurry of emotions washed over him – gratitude, guilt, and a sense of longing he hadn't noticed before.

"Please, forget I said anything," she whispered, wiping away a tear. "Just... promise me you'll think about what I said."

"Of course," Tom murmured, unable to tear his gaze away from her face. As they sat in silence, the air between them thick with unspoken feelings and tension, it became clear that their journey together was far from over.

"Emma," Tom began tentatively after a few moments, "I appreciate your honesty and everything you've done for me. I promise I'll think about what you said."

"Thank you," Emma replied quietly, her gaze meeting his, a mix of vulnerability and strength in her eyes.

"Maybe we should take a break from planning the grand gesture for Serena. Just for a little while," he suggested, thinking that it might help both of them to have some time apart and gain clarity on their feelings.

"Maybe that's for the best," she agreed, nodding slowly. They sat there for a moment, knowing that they were on the precipice of something uncharted, but neither daring to take the plunge.

"Emma, can I ask you something?" Tom inquired, his voice wavering slightly.

"Of course," she responded, steeling herself for whatever question he might have.

"Have you ever... felt like this before? Like there's so much left unsaid, but you're afraid to say it because it might change everything?"

"Tom, I..." Emma hesitated, her heart pounding in her chest. She knew the answer, but saying it out loud could potentially alter the delicate balance they had established between friendship and something deeper.

"Sorry, I shouldn't have asked," Tom quickly backtracked, recognizing the discomfort on her face.

"No, it's okay. It's just... difficult to put into words," Emma admitted, exhaling softly. "But yes, I've felt like this before."

"Me too," Tom confessed, this is how I feel about Serena, now do you understand why I have to finish this?

"Ah, I see," Emma tried to hide her disappointment, feeling a pang in her chest.

"Hey," Tom reached out and gently placed his hand on her arm. "I hope you know how much I appreciate everything you've done for me. Your support has meant the world."

"Of course, Tom," Emma forced a smile, trying to mask her true feelings. "You're my friend, and I want you to be happy."

"Thanks," Tom said sincerely, looking into her eyes and sensing that there was still more left unsaid between them. "Well, we should get back to planning your grand gesture, right?"

"Right," Emma agreed reluctantly, trying to focus on the task at hand rather than the storm of emotions brewing inside her.

Together, they resumed their plans for winning Serena back, but the tension between them remained palpable. As the chapter drew to a close, the emotional turmoil between Tom and Emma hung heavy in the air, leaving both of them questioning their unspoken feelings for one another and setting the stage for the next chapter's resolution.

As Tom and Emma continued their planning, the atmosphere between them grew more and more tense. The weight of their unspoken feelings made every interaction feel strained, with lingering glances and hesitant touches leaving each of them feeling breathless and uncertain.

"Okay," Tom said, trying to focus on the task at hand. "I think I have a good idea for a grand romantic gesture. What do you think about a hot air balloon ride over the city at sunset?"

"Wow," Emma replied, her heart skipping a beat as she imagined herself in that scenario with Tom. "That sounds...incredible."

"Right?" Tom grinned, his enthusiasm momentarily pushing aside the tension between them. "I just need to figure out how to make it perfect, you know? Something that will really show Serena how much I've changed and that I'm worth giving another chance."

"Tom," Emma hesitated, biting her lip as she considered her next words carefully. "Do you think this is what Serena would actually want? Or are you doing this to prove something to yourself?"

"Emma, I..." Tom trailed off, unsure of how to answer her question. In truth, he had never stopped to consider if this was what Serena would truly want. But the thought of backing down now was simply unthinkable.

"Look, I just want to be the best version of myself for her," Tom finally said, his voice filled with determination. "If she can see how much effort I've put into becoming a better man, maybe she'll give me another chance."

"Maybe," Emma echoed quietly, her heart aching with the knowledge that she might lose Tom forever if his plan succeeded. She couldn't help but wonder if he would ever look at her the same way he looked at Serena.

"Anyway," Tom said, attempting to break through the heavy silence that had settled between them. "I should probably get going. I've got a lot to do before I head back to London."

"Of course," Emma nodded, forcing a smile. "Good luck with everything, Tom. I really hope it all works out for you."

"Thank you, Emma," Tom said sincerely, his gaze lingering on her face for a moment longer than necessary. "I couldn't have done any of this without you."

As they parted ways, the emotional turmoil between them remained unresolved, leaving both Tom and Emma grappling with their feelings and setting the stage for a potentially life-changing confrontation in the next chapter.

The next day, Tom marched into the gym with single-minded purpose. He headed straight for the free weights, ready to push his body to the brink. As he began his workout, emotions churned within him - determination, heartache, and confusion after his tense conversation with Emma.

With each repetition, Tom grunted and strained, using the exertion to clear his mind. Weights clanked loudly as he slammed them onto the floor after each set, eliciting alarmed glances from other gym members.

"Take it easy, pal," a bulky, bald-headed man called out. "Those weights didn't do anything to you."

Tom smiled sheepishly, wiping the sheen of sweat from his brow. "Sorry, guess I'm working through some stuff today."

As Tom moved through his workout, pangs of guilt tugged at his heart whenever he thought of Emma. He couldn't understand why she had reacted so strongly against his plans to win back Serena.

Did Emma resent him for needing her help? Or was there another, deeper reason she seemed to disapprove of his romantic gesture? Tom's mind spun as he considered the possibilities.

Lost in thought, he wandered over to the treadmills. Hopping onto the nearest one, Tom cranked it up to an aggressive pace, hoping the rhythmic pounding of his feet would drown out the uncertainty in his mind.

Other gym members shot him bemused glances as his arms flailed wildly with each stride. Tom's face scrunched in comic determination as he pushed himself faster, nearly toppling over in the process.

"Whoa there!" A petite blonde woman yelled out. "Might want to slow it down before you fly off and smack into a mirror."

"Roger that!" Tom called back cheerfully, reducing his frantic pace to a light jog. As the treadmill slowed, he felt his racing mind begin to calm as well. Tom knew he needed to have an open and honest discussion with Emma to clear the air between them.

After the workout, Tom freshened up and headed to Emma's apartment, rehearsing what he would say along the way. When she opened the door, surprise flickered across her striking features.

"Tom! I wasn't expecting to see you today," Emma said, tucking a loose strand of raven hair behind her ear self-consciously.

"Sorry for dropping by unannounced," Tom apologized. "But I was hoping we could talk."

"Of course, come on in," Emma stepped aside, her heartbeat quickening nervously.

As Tom settled onto the plush gray couch in Emma's living room, she could feel her heartbeat quickening nervously. She knew this was the moment she had to reveal her true feelings, no matter how vulnerable it made her.

"So..." Emma began, perching on the edge of the armchair across from Tom. "What did you want to talk about?"

Tom took a deep breath before speaking. "I just want to clear the air after our conversation yesterday. I feel like there's something you're not telling me, and it's created this...tension between us."

Emma inhaled sharply, her shoulders tensing. This was her chance, but as she looked into Tom's earnest green eyes, all she could think about was how focused he was on winning back Serena.

"Tom, I..." she started hesitantly. But the words caught in her throat. How could she tell him how she really felt when he was so set on that romantic gesture for another woman?

Sensing her discomfort, Tom reached out and gave her hand a supportive squeeze. "Emma, you know you can tell me anything. I trust you."

Blinking back tears, Emma forced a smile. "It's nothing, really. I guess I've just been stressed about work and took it out on you unfairly when we talked about your plans yesterday. I'm sorry."

The lie tasted bitter on her tongue, but she couldn't bring herself to confess her feelings and risk Tom's rejection. She had to keep pretending, for both their sakes.

"Hey, it's okay. No need to apologize," Tom said kindly. "I know you've always got my back."

Emma's heart ached, but she maintained her composure. "Of course. What are friends for?"

She stood up abruptly, feigning a cheerful demeanor. "Now, how about I make us some tea?"

"That would be great, thanks," Tom replied, though his brows were still furrowed with mild concern.

As Emma busied herself in the kitchen, she blinked back tears, berating herself for her cowardice. But what choice did she have? Tom deserved to find happiness with Serena, even if it broke Emma's heart in the process. She could never be the one to stand in the way of that.

So Emma resolved to swallow her feelings and continue supporting Tom as a friend. Even if doing so meant silently yearning for a love she could never have. Their journey would go on, but the words left unspoken would forever linger between them, a bittersweet ache in her heart.

Chapter 4 Awakening Feelings

Tom stood in Emma's sunlit kitchen, a somber look on his face as he hesitated to reveal his upcoming departure. He shifted his weight from one foot to the other, trying to find the right words.

"Emma," he began, his voice barely above a whisper, "I've decided to go back to London in a week to put my plan with Serena into action." Tom braced himself for her reaction, knowing how important their time together had become.

Emma's heart sank like a stone at the mention of Serena's name. She felt an unexpected pang of jealousy and dread at the thought of losing Tom. Yet, she knew she had to keep her emotions in check. Taking a deep breath, she mustered up a smile and said, "Well, we'll just have to make this last week an amazing one, won't we?"

That evening, Emma surprised Tom with a homemade healthy dinner, having taken note of his favorite nutritious foods during their time together. She carefully prepared quinoa salad with grilled vegetables, avocado slices, and a side of fresh fruit, ensuring it was not only delicious but also wholesome.

"Wow, Emma, this looks incredible!" Tom exclaimed, unable to hide his delight at her thoughtfulness. "I can't believe you went through all this trouble for me."

"Of course," Emma replied, trying to sound casual. "I know how hard you've been working, and I wanted to do something special for you."

Tom grinned, his green eyes crinkling at the corners as he looked at Emma. "Thank you, Emma. You really are amazing, you know that?" He was genuinely touched by her gesture but remained oblivious to the deeper feelings behind it.

As they sat down to enjoy the meal together, Emma couldn't help but think about what her life would be like without Tom's smiling face and infectious laughter filling her days. She tried to shake off her melancholy thoughts, reminding herself that she had one more week to make an impact on Tom's life before he returned to London.

"Emma," Tom said suddenly, snapping her back to reality. "I just want you to know how grateful I am for everything you've done for me. You've helped me see my own potential, and that means more to me than you'll ever know."

Emma felt a warmth spread through her chest as she met Tom's gaze. She knew that no matter what happened with Serena, she would always cherish the time they spent together and the bond they had formed.

"Thank you, Tom," she replied softly, her eyes shining with unshed tears. "That means a lot to me."

"Anyway," Emma said, clearing her throat and wiping away the hint of a tear, "I have another surprise for you. Tomorrow, I've planned an outdoor activity that I think you'll love."

"Really?" Tom asked, his curiosity piqued. "What is it?"

"Ah, not so fast!" Emma replied playfully. "It's a surprise, remember? But I can tell you this much: it involves the beautiful California coast."

"Sounds exciting," Tom said, grinning. "I can't wait!"

The following day, Emma led Tom to a scenic spot overlooking the ocean, where they rented bikes to ride along the breathtaking coastal trail. The sun was shining brilliantly, casting a warm golden light on the crashing waves below.

"Wow, Emma, this is incredible!" Tom exclaimed as they began their ride, the salty sea breeze tugging at their hair. "I had no idea places like this existed in California."

"Sometimes it's good to get out of the gym and experience the world around us," Emma said, smiling. "There's nothing quite like the great outdoors to remind us of our place in the grand scheme of things."

As they rode together, Tom couldn't help but be impressed by Emma's adventurous spirit. Her enthusiasm for life seemed to be contagious, and he found himself laughing and joking with her more than he had with anyone else in years. He felt a growing connection with her, something that went beyond their shared passion for fitness and self-improvement.

"Emma," Tom said as they paused to catch their breath and take in the stunning view, "I just want to say thank you again. This has been one of the best weeks of my life, and it's all thanks to you."

"Tom," Emma replied, her voice thick with emotion, "you've changed my life too. I'm so glad we met, and I hope that even after you go back to London, we'll always stay friends."

"Of course," Tom agreed, his own eyes glistening with unspoken feelings. "You're an amazing person, Emma Sullivan, and I'm lucky to have you in my life."

As the sun began to set over the ocean, casting a warm orange glow across the sky, Emma and Tom rode on, side by side, their hearts full of gratitude and an undeniable connection that neither could ignore any longer.

The next day, Emma woke up early with a mission on her mind. She wanted to make sure Tom knew just how much he meant to her and how proud she was of the progress he had made. So, she decided to leave little notes of encouragement for him to find throughout the day.

"Morning, sunshine!" she greeted him cheerfully as they met up for their daily workout. "I made you a protein shake to get your energy levels up."

"Thank you, Emma," Tom replied, surprised by her thoughtfulness. "You really didn't have to do that."

"Of course I did," Emma said with a smile. "Now, let's get started!"

As the day went on, Tom began to discover Emma's carefully placed notes. He found one tucked into his gym bag, which read, "You're stronger than you think, Tom! Keep pushing yourself." Another note was attached to his water bottle, saying, "Remember to stay hydrated – it's the key to success!" Each note brought a smile to his face and a warmth to his heart.

Tom couldn't believe how much effort Emma had put into making him feel special and appreciated. He had always known that she was an extraordinary person, but these small acts of kindness showed him just how deeply she cared for him. And as he read each note, he felt something stirring within him – a realization that maybe, just maybe, Emma was more than just a friend.

"Hey Emma," Tom called out later that afternoon, after finding another note hidden inside his favorite book. "I found your notes. Thank you so much – they mean a lot to me."

"Good, I'm glad they made you smile," Emma replied with a grin. "I wanted to make sure you know how much progress you've made and that I believe in you. Now, I have another surprise for you."

"Another one?" Tom asked, his curiosity piqued.

"Yep! I got us tickets to a comedy show tonight. I know how much you love to laugh, and I thought it would be a great way to unwind after all the hard work you've been putting in," Emma explained, her brown eyes sparkling with excitement.

"Wow, Emma, that sounds amazing! Thank you so much," Tom exclaimed, genuinely touched by her thoughtfulness.

As they settled into their seats at the comedy club, Tom couldn't help but steal glances at Emma. He noticed the way her eyes crinkled when she laughed, and the warmth of her hand as it brushed against his when they both reached for a drink. The more time he spent with her, the more he found himself drawn to her, like a moth to a flame.

The show was hilarious, and Tom hadn't laughed so hard in years. As the comedian cracked jokes about dating mishaps and gym faux pas, Tom felt an overwhelming sense of gratitude for having Emma by his side. She had brought joy back into his life when he needed it most, and he couldn't imagine facing the rest of his journey without her.

During a particularly uproarious bit, Emma leaned over, her laughter contagious, and whispered in Tom's ear, "See? Laughter really is the best medicine."

Tom nodded, smiling broadly. "You're absolutely right, Emma. Thank you for this incredible evening." His green eyes met her brown ones, and for a moment, time seemed to stand still. And although neither of them said it out loud, they both knew that their connection went far beyond shared laughter and a mutual love for health and fitness.

The next day, Emma decided to up the ante in her quest to make their last week together unforgettable. She organized a group workout session at a local park, inviting some of the friends Tom had made during his time in California. As they gathered on the grassy field under the warm sun, Emma hoped that the camaraderie and support of these new relationships might persuade Tom to stay.

"Alright, everyone," Emma called out as she clapped her hands together, her athletic frame radiating confidence. "Today's workout is all about teamwork and motivation. We're in this together!"

Tom looked around at the familiar faces – people who had become like a second family to him over the past few months – and felt a surge of determination. He didn't want to let them down, but more importantly, he didn't want to let Emma down. He could see the effort she had put into organizing this event, and it stirred something within him.

"Let's do this!" Tom shouted enthusiastically, earning cheers from the group. As the workout progressed, he found himself pushing harder than ever before, motivated by the energy and encouragement of those around him. Sweat dripped down his face as he performed burpees, squats, and lunges in unison with the others, but he refused to give up.

Emma watched Tom with a mix of pride and admiration. He had come so far since they first met, not just physically but mentally as well. His newfound resilience and dedication were inspiring, and she couldn't help but be drawn to the man he was becoming.

"Great job, everyone!" Emma called out as they finished the last set of exercises. "And a special shoutout to Tom for giving it his all today." The group applauded, and Tom flushed with pride.

"Thanks, Emma," he said, wiping the sweat from his brow. "I couldn't have done it without you – or any of you," he added, gesturing to the group. "You've all made my time here in California truly special."

As they all exchanged hugs and high-fives, Emma couldn't help but feel a pang of sadness. She knew that their time together was running out, and despite her best efforts, she still wasn't sure if she had done enough to make Tom reconsider his plans. But as she looked into his eyes, she saw something that gave her hope – a flicker of doubt, a spark of possibility.

The warm California sun cast a golden haze over the bustling farmer's market as Emma led Tom through the maze of vibrant stalls. The air was filled with the scent of fresh herbs, ripe fruit, and the earthy aroma of vegetables pulled straight from the soil.

"Wow, this place is amazing!" Tom exclaimed, his green eyes wide with wonder as he took in the array of colorful produce. "I had no idea there were so many different types of fruits and vegetables."

Emma grinned, her brown eyes twinkling with excitement. "That's the beauty of a farmer's market, Tom. You get to discover new foods that you might not find at your regular grocery store. Plus, everything is fresher and more flavorful. It makes all the difference when cooking healthy meals."

As they walked from stall to stall, Emma enthusiastically introduced Tom to various ingredients, explaining the nutritional benefits and offering tips on how to incorporate them into his diet. Tom listened intently, eager to learn and expand his culinary horizons.

"Try this," Emma said, handing him a slice of juicy mango. He took a tentative bite, a look of pure delight spreading across his face as the sweet flavor exploded on his tongue.

"That's incredible!" he declared, reaching for another piece. "Why have I never tried this before?"

"Life is full of delicious surprises," Emma replied with a wink, enjoying the way Tom embraced each new experience with enthusiasm.

After collecting an assortment of fresh ingredients, they returned to Emma's apartment, where she guided Tom through the process of preparing a simple yet scrumptious meal. Together, they chopped, sautéed, and seasoned their way to a mouthwatering feast.

"Okay, moment of truth," Emma announced as they sat down to eat. Tom took a bite, savoring the flavors and textures that danced on his taste buds.

"Emma, this is incredible!" he said, genuinely impressed. "I didn't know healthy food could taste so good."

She smiled warmly, her heart swelling with pride. "That's the magic of cooking with fresh ingredients and a little bit of love. Food can be both nutritious and delicious if you give it a chance."

As they enjoyed their meal, Tom couldn't help but marvel at the transformation he had undergone since meeting Emma. Not only had his body changed, but his entire outlook on life had shifted as well. He felt stronger, healthier, and more alive than ever before – and he owed it all to the determined, passionate woman sitting across from him.

"Emma," he began, pausing to gather his thoughts. "I just want you to know how grateful I am for everything you've done for me. You've opened my eyes to a whole new world, and I can't thank you enough."

"Tom, it's been my pleasure," she replied, her voice soft with emotion. "Seeing you grow and change has been one of the most rewarding experiences of my life."

As they locked gazes, Tom saw a hint of vulnerability in her eyes – a glimpse into the depth of her feelings for him.

The morning sun cast a warm glow on the small wooden table by the window, where Emma carefully crafted her heartfelt letter to Tom. With each stroke of her pen, she poured her admiration and feelings onto the paper, hoping that somehow, it would be enough to convey the depth of her emotions.

"Tom," she began, "I know you're leaving soon, and I can't help but feel like there's something important I need to tell you."

She paused, wondering how to phrase her thoughts without revealing too much.

"Throughout our time together, I've watched you grow and change in ways I never could have imagined. Your determination, resilience, and unwavering commitment to becoming the best version of yourself have inspired me more than I can say. And it's with immense pride and joy that I've been able to witness your transformation."

Emma hesitated, her heart pounding as she found the courage to hint at her deeper feelings.

"Though our journey may be coming to an end, I want you to know that you'll always have a special place in my heart. And no matter what the future holds, I'll be cheering you on every step of the way."

With a deep breath, she signed her name and sealed the envelope, slipping it into Tom's gym bag when he wasn't looking.

Later that day, as Tom rummaged through his bag for a water bottle, his hand brushed against something unexpected. Curious, he pulled out the envelope and unfolded the letter, his eyes scanning the words that Emma had penned with such care.

As he read, his heart swelled with emotion, overwhelmed by the love and support that radiated from the page. He hadn't realized just how deeply Emma cared for him until now, and the revelation left him feeling both elated and confused.

"Is it possible?" he wondered, his mind racing with questions. "Could she really have feelings for me? Tom thought about it and came to the conclusion that she was a great friend and wanted him to know that and if he pursue asking her if this was more than friendship, then he could ruin it forever and that would not be worth losing her over.

The week came to an end faster than either of them had anticipated, and it was time for Tom to return to London. With a heavy heart, Emma drove him to the airport, trying her best to remain cheerful despite the sadness that threatened to consume her.

"Thanks for everything, Emma," Tom said as they stood outside the terminal, his green eyes filled with gratitude and a hint of sorrow. "I don't think I could've done any of this without you."

"Of course," she replied, forcing a smile. "You're stronger than you think, Tom. Just remember everything we've worked on together, and you'll be fine."

They shared one last hug, and Emma watched as Tom disappeared through the airport doors, clutching the letter she had written to him tightly in his hand. She stayed until the plane was no longer visible in the sky, a single tear rolling down her cheek as she waved goodbye.

Emma cried all the way home, unable to contain the emotions that had been building inside her over the last week. Upon arriving at her apartment, she was confronted by her best friend, who had been waiting anxiously for her return.

"Emma, what's wrong?" her friend asked, concern evident in her voice.

"Tom... he left for London today," Emma choked out between sobs. "And I never told him how I truly feel about him."

Her best friend shook her head, exasperated. "You idiot! You let him go without telling him? You have to go after him, Emma! It's not too late!"

But Emma hesitated, her brown eyes filled with uncertainty. "What if he doesn't feel the same way? What if I ruin our friendship?"

"Sometimes, taking a risk is worth it," her friend insisted, placing a comforting hand on Emma's shoulder. "You'll never know unless you try, and I have a feeling he might feel the same way about you."

With her friend's words echoing in her mind, Emma wiped away her tears and made a decision. She would go after Tom, chase after the possibility of love and happiness that had been right in front of her all along. She didn't want to live with the regret of never knowing what could have been.

"Alright," she said, determination lighting up her face. "I'll do it. I'll go after him."

"Good," her friend smiled, giving her a supportive hug. "Now let's book you a flight to London!"

Chapter 5 Chasing Dreams

Tom Hawthorne's heart pounded with excitement as he stepped off the plane in London. The city seemed to glow with an ethereal light, like a dream come true after his transformative journey. Gone were the days of neglecting his appearance and doubting himself; he was ready to face life head-on.

"Alright," Tom whispered to himself, running a hand through his newly groomed brown hair. "Let's do this."

He pulled out his phone, hesitating for just a moment before sending a message to Serena Davis, his ex-girlfriend. "Hey Serena, I'm back in town. We need to meet up – I have so much to tell you and some things to show you." He hit send, his green eyes sparkling with determination.

"Really, Tom? You think she'll care?" The voice of doubt nagged at him, but he pushed it away, knowing that change had made him stronger than ever before.

To his surprise, Serena's reply came within minutes. "Fine, I can meet you at Café Chic in the city center. But it better be worth my time."

"Alright! It's a date!" Tom couldn't help but grin as he typed his response, though he knew deep down that his feelings for Serena didn't compare to those he felt for Emma. Still, he had a plan, and meeting Serena was the first step.

Café Chic was bustling with the typical London crowd when Tom arrived, his newfound confidence evident in the way he strode through the door. He scanned the room, searching for Serena's familiar face among the sea of strangers.

The vibrant hum of the bright blue convertible Lamborghini reverberated through the busy London streets, turning heads as it pulled up outside the trendy café. Tom sat behind the wheel, his heart racing with a mixture of excitement and anxiety. He couldn't help but feel a sense of pride in his transformation, both mentally and physically. But there was one more person he needed to see before he could truly move on.

"Alright, Tom," he muttered to himself, taking one last steadying breath. "This is it."

He stepped out of the car, his newly toned physique and well-groomed appearance drawing admiring glances from passersby. For once, he didn't shy away from the attention - instead, he embraced it, standing tall and confident.

"Focus," he reminded himself, scanning the outdoor seating area for Serena. His green eyes soon found her, engrossed in her phone as she sat at a small table near the entrance. She had yet to notice his arrival, giving him a moment to take in her beauty – the wavy brunette hair, the hazel eyes that used to captivate him so easily. But now, something felt different – hollow even.

"Serena?" Tom called out softly, approaching her table with an easy grin.

Her head snapped up, eyes widening in surprise as they took in the sight before her. The once unkempt brown-haired man she'd left behind had transformed into this striking figure, exuding confidence and charm.

"Tom? Is that really you?" Serena stammered, momentarily speechless. Her gaze flicked back and forth between him and the luxurious car parked nearby. "What happened to you?"

"Hey," he replied amiably, trying to keep his nerves in check. "I've been working on myself, inside and out. It's been quite the journey."

"Clearly," Serena said, her voice tinged with disbelief as she looked him up and down once more. "You look… amazing."

"Thanks," Tom said, his smile genuine but a little sad. He couldn't help but think of Emma – her warmth, her laughter, her unwavering belief in him – and realized that it was her he wanted to share this moment with.

He sat down across from Serena, knowing that the time had come to face the past and fully embrace his future. But first, he needed to have this conversation – one last hurdle before he could truly be free.

"Serena, there's something I need to tell you."

"Go on," Serena urged, leaning in with curiosity.

Tom took a deep breath and smiled, fully aware of the life-changing revelation he was about to share. "I'm in love with someone else."

"Who?" Serena's eyes narrowed, her mouth still agape from the shock of Tom's transformation.

"Her name's Emma," Tom said, his heart swelling with warmth as he spoke her name. "She's amazing, Serena. She helped me become the person I am today – the person I've always wanted to be."

Serena blinked, trying to process the information. Her lips were still parted in astonishment, but her gaze held a flicker of something else – perhaps envy or disappointment.

"Emma," she repeated, almost bitterly.

"Emma," Tom confirmed, smiling wider than ever. "And I need to go to her right now."

He reached out and gently placed a hand on either side of Serena's face, pulling her towards him for a tender goodbye kiss. As their lips met, he realized that any lingering feelings he had for her had vanished completely. His heart belonged to Emma, and it was time to let go of the past.

"Goodbye, Serena," he whispered softly, before standing up and turning on his heel to leave the café.

The world seemed to blur around him as he sprinted back to the waiting Lamborghini, his heart pounding with excitement and anticipation. He started the car and roared off, racing through the streets of London towards his parents' house.

"Mom! Dad!" Tom shouted as he burst through the front door, startling Caroline and Peter Hawthorne from their afternoon tea. "I'm in love with Emma, and I need you both to come to California with me so you can meet her!"

Caroline and Peter exchanged knowing glances, their faces lighting up with joy at their son's happiness. They'd always hoped he would find someone who truly made him happy, and it seemed that Emma was the one.

"Of course, Tom!" Caroline exclaimed, rising from her seat. "We'll pack our bags right away!"

"California, here we come!" Peter chimed in, his smile almost as wide as Tom's.

The three of them raced around the house, gathering clothes, passports, and other essentials for their whirlwind journey across the Atlantic. Laughter bubbled up around them, punctuating the chaotic energy that filled their home as they prepared to catch the next flight to California.

"Emma," Tom whispered under his breath, clutching his plane ticket tightly in his hand. "I'm coming for you."

Meanwhile, on the other side of the world, Emma paced nervously outside the ticket counter at the California airport. Her best friend stood beside her, both of them determined to secure a flight to London as quickly as possible.

She kept glancing at the clock, wondering if she was making a huge mistake chasing after Tom like this.

What if he didn't actually have feelings for her and she was misreading all the signals? The thought of putting her heart on the line and being rejected made her stomach churn nervously.

"Come on, we need to get to that counter!" Emma urged, her striking brown eyes filled with determination. She was anxious to see Tom again and didn't want to waste another moment apart from him.

"Excuse me, pardon me," her best friend said, gently pushing people aside in the queue as they made their way to the front, lets get that ticket so you can sweep Tom off his feet!". Emma smiled weakly, her friend's confidence doing little to quell her fears. "I don't know if I'd say sweep him off his feet exactly..."

Emma laughed, shaking her head. "Sure, if real life was actually like the movies. But what if--"

Her friend cut her off, clasping a hand over Emma's mouth. "No what-ifs! We're doing this!

"Oh come on, where's that fiery trainer spirit?" her friend insisted, grabbing Emma by the shoulders. "You can do this! It'll be like, a real-life rom-com scene."

When they finally reached the counter, the attendant looked up and gave them a sympathetic smile.

"You've got this! Tom's going to be so excited when you show up!" she gushed, practically bouncing up and down.

The ticket agent checked the flight details and gave a concerned look to Emma. "Unfortunately, there's only one ticket left on the London flight, it's in first-class, and it's $8,000," she informed them, her voice apologetic.

"Eight thousand dollars?" Emma hesitated for a split second, but she knew that getting to Tom was worth any price. She exchanged a resolute look with her best friend, who nodded in agreement. They pooled their credit cards together and handed them over to the attendant, their hearts pounding with a mixture of excitement and anxiety.

"Thank you," Emma whispered as she clutched the precious ticket tightly. "London, here I come."

"Tom needs to know I'm coming," she murmured to her best friend, pulling out her phone and dialing his number. But try as she might, she couldn't get through to him. Frustrated, she sighed heavily. "I'll just have to surprise him."

"Sometimes surprises are the best way, Em," her best friend encouraged, giving her a reassuring hug before parting ways.

"Go get him!" her friend whispered, hugging Emma tightly.

With her heart in her throat, Emma handed the gate agent her ticket and disappeared down the jetway, hoping she wasn't making a terrible mistake.

The long flight gave Emma plenty of time to obsess over every possible scenario. What if Tom didn't even want to see her? Or worse - what if he had already reconnected with Serena? Emma stared out the window anxiously, her fingers drumming against her knees.

" Nervous flyer?" the kindly older woman next to her asked.

"Oh, uh, yeah...something like that," Emma stammered, realizing her inner turmoil must be written all over her face.

"Well, try not to worry dear," the woman said gently. "Everything will work out the way it's meant to be."

Emma smiled appreciatively, wishing she shared the woman's calm outlook.

As the plane began its descent into London, Emma's pulse quickened. This was it - the moment of truth. She had no idea what awaited her, but she knew it was time to take a leap of faith.

The bustling London airport was swarming with travelers racing to their destinations. Emma felt completely out of her element trying to navigate the busy terminals.

At the very same time, Tom boarded his flight from London to California, his heart pounded with anticipation. He couldn't wait to see Emma and tell her how he felt. At that very moment, Emma's plane touched down in London. As soon as her phone regained signal, she dialed Tom's number again, hoping against hope that she would reach him this time.

"Tom?" She breathed into the phone when he finally picked up, relief washing over her. "I'm in London, Tom. I'm sorry, but I love you and need to see you and tell you this."

"Emma!" Tom exclaimed, his voice filled with equal parts surprise and joy. "You won't believe this, but I'm on a plane about to leave for California – to tell you the same thing!"

"Tom, is there any way you can get off the plane?" Emma pleaded urgently, her heart sinking at the thought of missing him by mere moments.

"Emma, I don't think I can get off the plane," Tom admitted, feeling trapped and desperate as the doors closed and locked behind him.

"Oh yes, you can," his father interjected from the seat beside him. Without another word, Peter Hawthorne slipped out of his seat and feigned a heart attack, drawing the attention of the flight attendants and surrounding passengers.

"Medical emergency!" Caroline called out, playing her part in the ruse. Soon, paramedics arrived and began escorting Tom and his parents off the plane.

"Emma," Tom whispered into the phone, "I'm coming. We're getting off the plane."

"Really? I'll be waiting at arrivals for you," Emma replied, her voice filled with hope and love.

With his heart racing, Tom raced through the airport, each step bringing him closer to the woman he loved.

"Tom, just hurry!" Emma urged, her heart pounding as she paced back and forth in the arrivals area. She gripped her phone tightly, feeling nervous and excited all at once.

"Stay on the line, Emma. I'm almost there," Tom panted as he sprinted through the airport terminal, his parents trailing behind him, trying to keep up with his frantic pace.

"Gate A12... Gate A13..." Tom muttered under his breath, scanning the signs above him. "I've never run so fast in my life!"

"Neither have we," Caroline added breathlessly, exchanging a weary glance with Peter, who had made a dramatic recovery and jumped out of the paramedics wheel chair.

"Emma, are you still there?" Tom asked, his voice filled with anticipation.

"Wait, I see you!" Emma exclaimed suddenly, her eyes locking onto Tom's figure as he rounded the corner into the arrivals area. She quickly ended the call and shoved her phone into her pocket.

"Emma!" Tom called out, catching sight of her at last. Their eyes met across the crowded airport, and for a moment, it felt like time stood still.

"Tom!" Emma cried, tears welling up in her eyes as she started running towards him.

"Emma!" Tom echoed, his heart swelling with love and joy as he sprinted to meet her.

As they reached each other, Tom swept Emma into his arms, their lips meeting in a passionate, loving kiss. The chaos of the bustling airport faded away, leaving only the two of them, wrapped up in their newfound love.

"Emma, I love you," Tom whispered, gazing into her warm brown eyes.

"I love you too, Tom," Emma replied softly, her hand resting gently on his cheek.

Caroline and Peter, both red-faced and slightly disheveled from their own frantic race, came to a stop just behind their son, watching the scene unfold before them with teary-eyed smiles. Caroline and Peter shared a knowing glance, their hearts full of happiness for their son and the woman he had come to love.

"Peter," Caroline whispered, clutching her husband's arm, "we knew it. We knew they were meant for each other."

"Yes, my love," Peter agreed, his voice filled with pride and happiness. "It looks like our boy has finally found his match."

As Tom and Emma's lips finally parted, they gazed into each other's eyes, their souls intertwining in a way that could never be undone.

"Emma," Tom murmured, his voice thick with emotion, "I can't imagine my life without you. You've changed me for the better, and I want to spend the rest of my days making you as happy as you've made me."

"Tom," Emma replied, her brown eyes shining with unshed tears, "I feel the same way. We were destined to find each other, and now that we have, I'm never letting go."

And as they embraced once more, surrounded by the bustling airport crowd, Tom and Emma knew that their love story was just beginning - an adventure that would take them through the peaks and valleys of life, hand in hand, hearts forever entwined.

Chapter 6 The Adventure Continues

The first rays of morning sunlight filtered through the lace curtains, casting a warm glow across the cozy breakfast nook. Emma, still adjusting to the time difference, sat sleepily across the table from Tom's parents, Peter and Caroline. The aroma of freshly brewed coffee and sizzling bacon filled the air as Caroline busied herself in the kitchen, humming a cheerful tune.

Peter, unable to take his eyes off Emma, grinned like a proud father-in-law-to-be. "I must say, Emma," he began, his voice thick with emotion. "We've heard so much about you, but seeing you here, with our boy... well, it's just splendid."

"Thank you, Mr. Hawthorne," Emma replied, blushing slightly. She couldn't help but smile at the thought of her whirlwind journey, flying first-class on six different credit cards just to tell Tom she loved him.

Caroline set down a plate piled high with scrambled eggs, toast, and bacon. "Now, dig in, everyone!" she said, her blue eyes twinkling with happiness. "And no more of this Mr and Mrs Hawthorne, it's mom and dad to you Emma."

As they all began to eat, Tom reached for Emma's hand under the table, giving it a gentle squeeze. "Emma, last night was incredible," he whispered, his green eyes filled with love. "I can't believe we're finally here, together."

"Me neither," Emma agreed, her heart swelling with affection. "I wouldn't have missed this for the world, Tom."

"Tom," Caroline interjected, sensing the deep connection between the two. "Why don't you tell Emma about that little place you used to love near Hampstead? I know you two have big dreams, and it might be perfect for what you have in mind."

Tom cleared his throat, his face flushing with excitement. "Well, it's this charming house with a beautiful garden – I always thought it would be a great place to live someday."

"Sounds lovely," Emma murmured, imagining the cozy space they could create together. "Maybe we should check it out?"

"Definitely," Tom agreed, his heart racing at the thought of building a life with Emma.

As they continued eating breakfast, Tom and Emma began discussing the challenges they might face as a couple. "We come from different worlds," Emma pointed out, her voice laced with determination. "But that's not going to stop us from making this work."

"Exactly," Tom concurred, his gaze locked on Emma's beautiful brown eyes. "We'll navigate any obstacles together because we're stronger as a team."

"Besides," Peter chimed in, his warm smile never faltering. "You two have already overcome so much just to be here today. I believe you can handle anything life throws your way."

"Your dad's right," Caroline added, her eyes misting up with pride. "You two are a testament to the power of love and self-improvement. We couldn't be happier for you both."

Gratitude swelled in Tom's chest as he looked around the table at the people who meant the most to him. Despite the challenges that lay ahead, he knew that with Emma by his side and the unwavering support of his parents, they would conquer anything together. In that moment, surrounded by love and laughter, the future had never seemed brighter.

"Speaking of our future," Tom began, stealing a glance at Emma before continuing, "I've been thinking about what we could do together in London. You know, combining our passions to help people change for the better, mentally and physically."

Emma's eyes sparkled with excitement as she leaned in, eager to hear more. "I love that idea! We could really make a difference in people's lives."

"Exactly!" Tom exclaimed, feeling the fire of inspiration ignite within him. "We could find a place to live together and build a life doing what we both love."

"London will always have a special place in my heart," Emma admitted, her voice softening. "I would love to call it home."

"Then it's settled," Tom declared, his green eyes shining with determination. "How about we start looking for a cozy house in Hampstead? It's a neighborhood I'm sure you will adore, and it would be perfect for us."

Emma's face lit up with joy, her heart swelling with affection for Tom. "I couldn't think of a better place for us to start our journey together."

As they sat around the table, their hearts filled with hope and anticipation, Tom and Emma knew that they were on the verge of something truly magical. With every challenge they faced, they would grow stronger as a couple, forging an unbreakable bond that would see them through the trials and triumphs that lay ahead. Hand in hand, they would create a life built on love, laughter, and shared dreams – a life that would become the very foundation of their happiness.

"Here's to our future," Tom whispered, his fingers entwined with Emma's as they shared a tender smile across the breakfast table.

"Here's to us," Emma echoed, her brown eyes brimming with love and adoration.

Together, they moved forward, ready to embrace the adventure that awaited them in the charming streets of Hampstead and beyond.

Over the next few weeks, Tom and Emma had both fallen in love with the house Tom always dreamed of owning in Hampstead.

"Can you imagine us cooking breakfast together in this kitchen?" Emma asked Tom as they stood in a spacious, sunlit kitchen during their house tour.

"Absolutely," Tom replied with a grin. "And having friends over for dinner in that cozy living room, sharing stories and laughter late into the night."

As they visited the property several times, to be sure it was perfect, Tom and Emma envisioned the life they would build together. They could see themselves curled up on the couch, watching classic movies with a bowl of popcorn, or hosting lively barbecues in their garden with friends and family. The possibilities seemed endless, and they couldn't help but feel excited about the future.

Their dream house was on a quiet street lined with beautiful trees. It was a warm brick cottage with ivy climbing its walls, nestled behind the most romantic small white picket fence. The moment they stepped inside, they knew they had found something special.

"Tom, this is it," Emma whispered, her eyes wide with wonder as she took in the cozy living room, complete with a fireplace and built-in bookshelves. "This feels like home already."

"I couldn't agree more," Tom said, his heart swelling with happiness. "I can see us making so many memories here. And look at the garden! It's perfect for summer evenings, don't you think?"

Emma gazed out the window at the lush green space, filled with blooming flowers and a lovely little pond. She could almost hear the sound of laughter and the clink of glasses from future gatherings they would host. "It's absolutely perfect," she agreed.

As they continued their tour, each room seemed to hold more promise than the last. The spacious kitchen with its inviting breakfast nook, the light-filled bedrooms that would provide a sanctuary after long days, and the peaceful garden – it was everything they had hoped for.

"Let's make this our home," Tom said, his voice filled with conviction and love.

"Let's do it," Emma replied, her hand tightly clasped in his. With their hearts set on the charming house, they couldn't wait to begin the next chapter of their lives together, creating memories and building dreams in the cozy warmth of their new home.

The cozy ambiance of the restaurant enveloped Tom and Emma as they sat across from one another, cheeks flushed with excitement. Only hours earlier, their offer had been accepted on the charming cottage they could now call their own.

Tom raised his glass, the candlelight dancing in his eyes. "To our new home," he proclaimed, "and the life we'll build within its walls. I can't wait to wake up next to you every morning in our new bedroom and cook breakfast with you in our kitchen."

Emma's heart swelled, and she clinked her glass against his. "To lazy Sundays snuggled on the couch and movie nights by the fire," she added with a radiant smile. Their eyes locked, brimming with love and promise.

As the evening went on, laughter and stolen glances flowed between them. Tom took Emma's hand, gently caressing her fingers, as though he never wanted to let go.

When dessert arrived, Emma looked up to see Tom slipping gracefully from his chair and down to one knee beside her. Her breath caught in her throat as he pulled out a glittering diamond ring.

"My darling Emma," he began, gazing up at her adoringly. "You are the light of my life. With you by my side, I feel stronger, kinder, and more complete than I ever dreamed possible."

Tears of joy shimmered in Emma's eyes as Tom described his hopes for their future together - one filled with passion, laughter, and unwavering partnership. "Will you do me the greatest honor of becoming my wife?" he finally asked, his voice brimming with emotion.

"Yes!" Emma cried through happy tears. "A million times, yes!" Tom swept her into his arms and kissed her deeply as the restaurant erupted in applause around them. Their hearts soared with love and the promise of an incredible life ahead, together at last.

Over the next few weeks, Tom and Emma excitedly began the process of moving in. They spent days carefully packing up their belongings, reminiscing over keepsakes and mementos that told the story of their lives so far. The act of packing and unpacking was a beautiful reminder of how much they had grown individually and as a couple through their transformative journeys.

"Remember this?" Tom asked, holding up a worn-out pair of running shoes. "These were the first ones I bought when we started our fitness journey together."

Emma smiled fondly at the memory. "I remember, and look how far you've come since then. You've become an inspiration to others, Tom. I'm so proud of you."

"Couldn't have done it without you by my side," Tom replied, pulling her close for a tender kiss.

As they unpacked and settled into their new home, they discussed plans for the layout and decoration. Each room presented a blank canvas on which they could paint their own unique blend of styles and personalities.

"Let's make the living room cozy and inviting, with plenty of cushions and warm colors," Emma suggested, her eyes lighting up with enthusiasm.

"Great idea! And what about creating a little reading nook by the fireplace? We can add a comfy armchair, a soft throw blanket, and a small side table for tea or coffee," Tom added.

"Perfect!" Emma agreed, already envisioning herself curled up there with a good book on a lazy Sunday afternoon.

Together, they ventured out to local shops and markets, picking out furniture, artwork, and decorative pieces that reflected both their tastes. A vintage clock from an antique store, a vibrant painting from a street artist, and a set of handcrafted pottery all found their place within the walls of their new haven.

With each addition, the house slowly transformed into a beautiful reflection of their love and shared dreams. It became a sanctuary where they could grow together, face challenges, celebrate triumphs, and find solace in each other's arms.

"Here's to our new home and the life we'll build together," Tom said, raising a glass of wine one evening as they sat in their newly decorated living room, surrounded by flickering candlelight and the soft hum of a jazz record playing in the background.

"Cheers to us," Emma echoed, her eyes brimming with love and happiness as she clinked her glass against his. In that moment, they knew that this house had truly become their home, filled with warmth, laughter, and the promise of many unforgettable memories yet to come.

One evening, as they sat on the couch enjoying a homemade meal, Tom turned to Emma with a spark in his green eyes. "You know, I've been thinking a lot about our future recently. We've come such a long way together, and now that we're settled in this beautiful home, maybe it's time for us to take the next step."

"Are you talking about starting our business?" Emma asked, her brown eyes lighting up at the thought of their shared dream.

"Exactly," Tom nodded enthusiastically. "I think we're ready to make our mark on the world. Let's combine our passion for helping others achieve their goals and create a life coaching and fitness center right here in London."

"Tom, I couldn't agree more," Emma said, beaming at the prospect of working side by side with the man she loved while doing something they both believed in wholeheartedly. "We can help people find happiness and health while growing even closer ourselves."

Over the next few weeks, they dedicated themselves to finding the perfect location for their new venture. They spent countless hours researching potential spaces, visiting various properties, and discussing the best ways to design and equip the facility to suit their clients' needs.

Finally, they discovered a charming building in a bustling neighborhood, not far from their cozy home in Hampstead. With its large windows, exposed brick walls, and ample space for both therapy sessions and workout areas, it was everything they had envisioned and more.

"Can you believe it, Emma? This is really happening!" Tom exclaimed as they signed the lease on their new business premises.

As they embarked on this new chapter, their love and commitment only grew stronger. In the evenings, they'd return to their warm and inviting home, sharing stories of the day's successes and challenges over candlelit dinners. And as they lay entwined on their couch, they knew without a doubt that they had found their true calling – both in each other and in the work they had chosen to pursue together.

The life coaching and fitness center flourished under Tom and Emma's leadership, becoming a beacon of hope and inspiration for those seeking happiness, health, and personal growth. And within its walls, Tom and Emma discovered not only the joy of helping others but also the boundless depths of their own love, which continued to grow and evolve with every passing day.

"Tom, I'm worried about the rising rent prices," Emma confided one evening after a long day at work. "It's getting harder for us to keep up with all the expenses."

"Let's not panic just yet," Tom reassured her, taking her hands in his. "We've faced challenges before, and we've overcome them together. We'll find a way through this as well."

Determined to keep their dream alive, Tom and Emma spent countless hours brainstorming ways to generate additional income for the business. They introduced group classes, workshops, and special promotions but still struggled to make ends meet.

"Maybe we should consider relocating the center to a more affordable area?" Tom suggested one night as they lay awake, mulling over their options.

"Or perhaps we could offer online sessions and expand our reach," Emma countered thoughtfully. "There are so many people out there who could benefit from what we have to offer."

"Emma, that's brilliant!" Tom exclaimed, sitting up with renewed energy. "We can help even more people, and it won't require a physical location!"

The next few weeks were a whirlwind of activity as Tom and Emma explored new ways to grow their business online. They recorded videos, set up social media accounts, and built a website to showcase their services. And as their virtual presence expanded, so too did their client base.

"Tom, look at these numbers – we're reaching people from all over the world now!" Emma said excitedly, scrolling through their analytics dashboard. "Our hard work is paying off."

"None of this would be possible without you, Emma," Tom replied, wrapping his arms around her waist. "Together, we can overcome any obstacle."

As their business continued to thrive, Tom and Emma grew closer than ever. Through every challenge and setback, they learned to lean on each other for support, finding strength in their love and the knowledge that they were building not only a successful business but also a life filled with joy and shared dreams.

"Tom, I can't imagine going through all of this with anyone else," Emma whispered one night as they stood on their balcony, gazing at the twinkling lights of London.

"Neither can I, my love," Tom murmured, pulling her close. "Together, we'll always find our way."

Four years later, Tom and Emma's garden was ablaze with vibrant colors as they celebrated a warm summer day with Caroline and Peter. Laughter filled the air as they shared stories and memories, while their sleepy golden retriever, Daisy, snoozed contentedly in a patch of sunlight.

"Can you believe it's been four years since we moved in?" Emma remarked, holding their one-year-old daughter, Lily, in her arms. The little girl gurgled happily, reaching out to grasp at a butterfly that fluttered by.

"Time flies when you're having fun," Tom replied, smiling down at his wife and daughter. "And I wouldn't have wanted to spend these years with anyone else."

Caroline and Peter couldn't help but beam with pride as they watched their son and daughter-in-law interact. Their love and devotion to each other had only grown stronger over the years, and now, as grandparents, they couldn't have been happier with the life Tom and Emma had built together.

"Pass the salad, please," Peter requested, grinning at Emma. "I can't get enough of your homemade dressing."

"Of course, Dad," Emma said, passing the bowl to him. "But I can't take all the credit – Tom's been teaching me some of his culinary tricks."

"See? We make a good team, both in the kitchen and in life," Tom chimed in, giving Emma a playful wink.

As the sun began to dip lower in the sky, bathing the garden in a warm golden glow, Tom and Emma exchanged a knowing look. They had come so far on their journey, overcoming challenges together and finding strength in their love. And as they looked forward to their future, hand in hand, they knew they had found something truly special in each other – soulmates and true callings that would carry them through the rest of their lives.

"Emma, remember our first session together?" Tom asked, his green eyes twinkling with mischief as he reminisced.

"Of course, how could I forget? You thought I was going to make your life miserable," Emma responded with a laugh.

"Hey now, don't forget that you were pretty intimidating as a fitness coach," Tom countered playfully. "But you also showed me the importance of believing in myself, and for that, I'll always be grateful."

"Speaking of which," Peter chimed in, looking at Emma with admiration, "the transformation we've seen in our son since meeting you has been nothing short of incredible. We couldn't have asked for a better partner for him."

"Thank you, Dad," Emma replied, her cheeks flushing a rosy shade. "I feel so lucky to be part of this family."

"Cheers to that!" Caroline exclaimed, raising her wine glass in a toast.

As they clinked glasses, they all revealed in the sense of happiness and contentment that filled the air. The garden seemed to come alive with the sound of laughter, the scent of fresh flowers, and the soft rustle of leaves in the gentle breeze.

"Tom, I can't believe how much our lives have changed since we decided to take on this journey together," Emma said softly, her brown eyes shining with love.

"Neither can I, Em," Tom agreed, squeezing her hand affectionately. "But one thing's for sure: I wouldn't trade any of it for the world."

They gazed at each other for a moment before turning their attention back to the table, where their daughter was giggling at something Caroline had said. Surrounded by love and support from both family and friends, Tom and Emma knew that they had everything they needed to continue thriving in their personal lives.

And as the sun dipped below the horizon, casting a warm, orange glow over the garden, Tom and Emma's story served as a testament to the power of self-improvement, the importance of having supportive friends, and the transformative power of love.

THE END

Printed in Great Britain
by Amazon

39604891R00046